I0636382

Agnes L. Sadlier

Gretchen's Gift

A noble sacrifice - an original tale

Agnes L. Sadlier

Gretchen's Gift
A noble sacrifice - an original tale

ISBN/EAN: 9783337088514

Printed in Europe, USA, Canada, Australia, Japan

Cover: Foto ©Andreas Hilbeck / pixelio.de

More available books at **www.hansebooks.com**

GRETCHEN'S GIFT;

A NOBLE SACRIFICE.

An Original Tale.

BY

A. L. S.

NEW YORK:

D. & J. SADLIER & CO., 31 BARCLAY STREET.
MONTREAL 275 NOTRE DAME STREET.
—
1879.

GRETCHEN'S GIFT.

JAKOB DIETZ lived in the old stone house upon the hill, a crazy, rambling structure, which bowed and shook before the keen north wind as if imploring its mercy.

In former years it had not so desolate a look. Before the Revolutionary days, an honest, thrifty farmer tilled and sowed the yielding hillsides, and they rose from the meadow-land's green bosom teeming with rich produce. But war sent a trumpet-call throughout the land ; the farmer threw down his scythe, and hastened to a place in the ranks of those toilers for freedom, and the farm was tilled no longer.

Next, its stout old walls sheltered the British soldiers ; its long, low-roofed rooms rang to uproarious mirth and echoed their toasts of confusion to the rebels. It was during this time that the grand old forest-trees which had shaded it in summer, and shook so fiercely over it in winter, were hewn down wherever they obstructed the view, or, in fact, when it suited the caprice of its quondam owners.

A few years passed, and peace emerged from the discord of two nations and smiled with added beauty upon the victors. The interrupted tide of emigration again swept their hospitable shores, and from its elevated place the old house glared upon numerous homesteads rising in the midst of cultivated fields, but it alone remained empty. Its former owner never appeared to claim his own, and soon people began to fear and shun it as if something uncanny had claimed the old house for its awful dwelling. Thoughts begot by superstition grow marvellously fast into words, and soon become established truth to their propagators. Thus they listened with avidity to the following tale concerning the old house, which, old Robert Laird averred, had been told dozens of times at his father's fireside:

As often happened in those days of

strife, two brothers held different political opinions. The elder clung to the
faith of his father and was a Tory;
the younger joined the handful of
struggling colonists and fought under
Ethan Allen.   One day a small de-
tachment of his regiment, he among
the number, was surprised and cap-
tured by a party of British, among
whom was his brother.   The British
conducted their prisoners to the old
house, where they were stationed.

During the evening the sight of his
young brother captive, appealed to the
soldier's heart with all the power of
affection transmitted by one blood and
race, and at last, duty was forgotten.
He happened to be sentry that night.
Hastening to his brother's room, he

showed him a plan of escape, of which
the latter, after many arguments, consented to take advantage. As the
two, so strangely hurried together, so
strangely parted, were interchanging a
last " good-by," the warmth of which no
political opinions could dampen, they
were discovered. The sergeant in
command, a man notorious throughout
the army for brutality, sentenced the
elder brother to death, and he was ac-
cordingly hanged the next morning before the windows ; and to increase the
horror of this example to all future
offenders, his brother was forced to
view the awful scene, and it was not
until the quivering body had stilled for
ever, that a swoon mercifully obscured
his senses, which never returned. He

rose from a bed of sickness a harmless,
roving maniac, who haunted with me-
lancholy persistence the scene of the
awful spectacle during life, and, it was
believed, visited it from the other
world.

Such was the story, whether true or
false, which gave the place an ill-re-
pute, and, despite its choice situation,
prevented any purchaser from appear-
ing.   The wide wooden gates, through
which formerly the patient oxen passed
at sunset, hung broken from their
hinges, and there remained no trace of
the footpath made by hurrying feet so
long ago.   The low, heavy entrance-
door was covered with numberless
scales, like some mighty fish—records
of many violent assaults of wind and

weather.   Above in the eaves swallows
dwelt in colonies, and chirped forth the
only sound that broke the solitude.

Such was the appearance of the for-
saken homestead when, one cool morning in the early spring-time, two farm-
ers, on their way to market, beheld
about it signs of real work-a-day life.

An old man, with stooped shoulders
and long gray hair, was busily employ-
ed in repairing the gate.   A box of
tools lay near him, and a huge dog, of
magnificent proportions, lay stretched
at full length upon the grass a short
distance away.

The news that a tenant or buyer had
at last taken the house was confirmed
that evening, when eager, anxious eyes
saw a light stream out from the small

diamond-paned windows, and curiosity immediately boiled over to learn the name of the hardy purchaser.

Little by little it transpired that the new household consisted of but three persons—old Jakob Dietz, a middle-aged woman named Frederica, and little golden-haired Gretchen. Their names betrayed their nationality. It was surmised that the little one was the old man's grandchild, and Frederica her nurse. But further than this probability failed to support the thousand conjectures formed about the family. Each had his or her pet theory concerning them—one that the woman had been old Jakob Dietz's accomplice in some crime, for which, in order to escape detection, they had been forced

to flee their country; others that it
was he who had stolen little Gretchen
from noble parents, and had simply
hired the aged *frau* to take charge of
her.

One point all agreed on—that the
child was not theirs. Those who had
been fortunate enough to obtain a near
view declared that her eyes were as
blue as the summer skies, and her hair
of a shining golden color. Now, old
Jakob had a singularly repelling look;
his eyes were of the smallest size
compatible with sight, and of a
greenish gray color. And as for
old Frederica, she regarded one with
a pair of the keenest black orbs,
and from under her cap, although her
hair was fast turning gray, it might

be seen that its original color matched her eyes

But however cold or repelling either of little Gretchen's guardians were to the neighbors who sought to cultivate acquaintance, to her they were all love and tenderness. Little Gretchen's first remembrances were of being watched and tended by Frederica, of being soothed and caressed in baby troubles in the old man's arms. She remembered many a shifting scene in her young life. Now they lived in the noise and rush of a city, under the eternal shadow of a mighty church. Through the long, dim aisles she had wandered while Frederica told her beads before Our Blessed Lady's shrine, and had gazed wonderingly at the tender, loving piety of the beautiful faces, creations of some mighty master, that looked on her from above. And often the sound of low, soft music, as from some distant choir, would wake gently the solemn stillness, and it was then she loved it best. An indefinable sensation, half-happiness, half-pain, always stirred her heart almost to bursting when listening to music. Often, though vainly, she strove to explain it to Frederica. The good woman loved music, like all her nation, but she loved best that which rang so loudly to the lofty carved ceiling at High Mass. She thought the plaintive music too sad, and eagerly recommended Gretchen not to think of it when it had passed.

Then Gretchen remembered a jour-

ney, partly by water, and they dwelt
again in the busy city; but this time
there was no church near by. Frederica and herself were hurried along
through a mighty throng on the streets,
who spoke in a strange tongue. The
city was much larger and the people
seemed more busy. All day long the ·
numbers of passers-by seemed never to
diminish. Awhile they lived here, and
then embarked for a long journey on
the sea. Many, many days and nights
they sailed, until one morning she was
awakened by Frederica, who told her
their journey was finished on the sea,
and Gretchen, going on deck, saw that
the ship was moored at the docks of a
city. After a little delay they landed
and three days' journey brought them

to their present home. And soon
Gretchen loved the old house almost
as well as that in the quaint old German town of which she was always
reminding Frederica. She loved to
wander through its wide, low-ceiled
rooms, for she was perfectly fearless;
to climb gently to the windows and
watch the birds at work in the eaves;
or even to ascend by a ladder to the
roof and look about the country. Then,
in the long, quiet evenings, she would
tell her adventures to her loving lis-
teners.

After, when the long summer days
had come, she would call Fritz, the
great dog, who from his shady resting-
place would rise, and, shaking himself,
follow his little mistress over hill and

valley. About half a mile from the
house there was a spot which Gretchen
loved better than all others. Two
lofty hills rose to an equal height,
and between them was a gorge,
through which, in summer, a tiny
rivulet hastened down, growing as
it went, until it reached the table-
ground a good-sized brook; and here
Gretchen used to rest on the long,
deep grass and listen to its soft, low
murmur.

Afterwards Gretchen learned that
her little brook grew very formidable
in winter, when it came rushing down,
swollen with the great rains. The six
huge stones, of which two were almost
sufficient to choke it altogether now, it
then sometimes almost covered, and

had, indeed, once been known to do so completely.

Summer passed into autumn, winter with its long nights came, and spring, returning, brought again the day on which a year ago they had come to the old house. And so time passed, until seven years had come and gone and Gretchen had grown into a maiden of fourteen years. Yet so slight and frail was she, and of so small a stature, that she appeared much less. Still, in the long winter evenings she sat at the old man's feet and sang, and he instructed her with the manner and air of one who both knew and loved music well. A great and glorious voice he recognized as the child's birthright, and he cultivated the noble gift, although

each note woke memories of a bitter
past.   Once, indeed, he had bade her
sing no more that evening, and ab-
ruptly retired; and when Gretchen
questioned Frederica upon his strange
conduct, the old woman muttered something of her looking like her mother.

"Listen, then, Frederica," replied
Gretchen.   "I will sing no more to
him, since it moves him so deeply to
be reminded of her."

"Nein, nein!" replied the old woman, "that would be fine, indeed, to
to have him blame me then for mentioning her to you.   I mean not that,
either," she continued, seeing a strange
expression gather on the girl's face;
"only he loved her so much he has
not ever quite got over her loss, and

mentioning her name reminds him of her. So promise me, little one, that you will not speak of it to him."

Thus urged, Gretchen complied and appeared to forget the matter.

It was now the middle of January and the ground was covered with snow, which the intensely cold weather had frozen so as to afford splendid travel to sleighs. Frederica, therefore, determined to go over to H—— for some articles which were wanted for the house. She was detained longer than she expected, and the early night had fallen before the sound of bells told on the cold, crisp air that she had come. Gretchen flew to the door, threw it open and greeted the old nurse with as warm a welcome as if she had come from the North Pole.

After the old woman had removed her wrappings, she took from her pocket a letter and handed it to her master, saying: "Herr Jakob, this letter has been lying in the post-office for two weeks."

The old man, with a start, took it from her, and, tearing it open, began to read it eagerly.

Frederica meanwhile busied herself in placing upon the pine table, white as driven snow, the evening meal which Gretchen's deft fingers had prepared. During its progress the child questioned Frederica, and listened delighted to all the doings and sayings which went to make up the current

of news in a country town forty years
ago.

From his distant corner Fritz raised
himself slowly and with difficulty—for
he was now in the unkind grasp of old
age—and came over to the hearth, from
whence he looked at his young mistress with his soft, faithful brown eyes,
as if beseeching her not to forget him
in busy conversation.

Nor did she; for while Frederica
washed the Delft-ware and arranged it
again on the shelves above the table,
the young girl placed many a choice
bit on the platter and laid it before
him on the hearth, to his great satisfac-
tion.

Then, when the hearth was swept
and the fire stirred until its ruddy light

blazed high and bright, she came in
obedience to the old man's sign and
seated herself on the low stool at his
feet, and sang as he bade her a quaint
old German ballad.   But the weird,
slow music seemed for once to fall upon unheeding ears.   His eyes were
closed and his head bent with the air
of one who ponders deeply.   When
the song had ceased he leaned down
and took her face in both his hands,
and said :

"My little Gretchen, to-night thou
shalt sing no more to me, but I will tell
thee a tale of what will seem to thee
the olden time."

Generally at this proposition the
child's face had been used to flush with
delight and eagerness, but to-night, re-

membering the letter, together with the unusual **solemnity of the old man's** voice **and manner, she felt** troubled and **uneasy, and waited for his** words with dread.

"Little **Gretchen**," he began, in deep, sonorous tones, "**forty years ago there** came journeying **on** foot **to the** gates of a great city a poor unknown youth. **Ugly and repulsive,** his **one** sole **gift from the good God** was musical **genius, and he sought in** the crowded places **for** some skilful hand **to** spring back the massive lock which ig· norance kept upon the treasure. Many, **many a weary** day and sleepless night **tortured** his burning heart, and sus**pense grew** greater than he could bear, when at last one day, as he sat at Vesper service, weeping bitterly with the organ, which, too, seemed to wail in sadness, a hand touched his shoulder, and, looking up, he beheld an old man with deep, peaceful eyes and long gray beard sweeping his breast. He beckoned the youth to follow him, who obeyed, until they reached the quiet, deserted street, for it was now evening. Then, pausing, the stranger questioned him as to the cause of his grief, listened to the story of his hopes and failures with deep interest, and said: 'My poor youth, I am one of those you seek; my whole life has been devoted to music, and I now teach many pupils. Come to this address to-morrow before noon, and I will talk with you further.'

"Then, kindly pressing the youth's

hand, he quitted him and was soon lost
in the gathering evening shadows.

"The following day the young man
presented himself at the house indicat-
ed and was instantly admitted to the
professor's presence. One interview
sufficed to found a friendship that only
ceased with life. The old man loved
the youth because of his passionate
gratitude and the enthusiasm with
which he applied himself to the study
of his great art, and the younger
loved him as we love one who gives to
us the realization of our heart's desire.

"Time went on, and three years had
elapsed since his first meeting with the
capelmeister, when one day, as he sat
waiting in his master's house for his
coming, the door opened and a maiden

entered whom he rightly supposed to
be his benefactor's daughter Cicely.
Long plaits of shining golden hair fell
far below her waist, and her eyes were
deep and blue as one of our mountain
lakes. With a half-bashful but smiling
air she approached, and, having enquired his name, informed him that her father had left word that he could not return until late, but desired that he
should wait his coming. Nothing loath,
the young man obeyed, but Cicely, after having conversed for a short time,
disappeared, nor did he behold her
again until, her father having returned,
they were summoned to supper.

"Little by little the maiden became
more friendly and intimate in their
intercourse," but the youth strove to

smother in his heart the love he felt
for her. What possible claim, his reason urged, could he ever hope to gain
upon the affection of one so beautiful
and gifted as Cicely? When, kneeling
in the choir, he saw her rapt and inspired beauty as her voice floated high
above the rest in the grand chants
of High Mass, a tinge of awe mixed
with his love, as if he had set it on a
thing too holy. Thus for ten long
years his great patient affection dwelt
silent within the closed doors of his
heart, until there came a time when
the professor lay upon his death-bed,
and Cicely was soon to be alone in the
world. Then the voice of his love
broke silence. Cicely, in the midst of
her great grief, gave obedient consent

to her father's wish, and knelt by his
bedside as he clasped her hand in that
of his loved pupil, and with his last
breath blessed them.

"The pair thus strangely betrothed
were married without waiting for the
time allotted to mourning. The loss
sustained was almost as great in one
case as the other, for the daughter's
betrothed husband had loved her father with the love of a son, and it was
deemed better that the maiden should
have a protector as soon as possible;
therefore one morning in the early
summer they were married, and came
down the church steps to the old home
that Cicely loved so well.

"Four happy years followed, and
then another summer morning, when

the soft air came through the open
lattice, sweet with the fragrance of
roses, her husband knelt by Cicely,
and heard her dying words as she
thanked him in low, weak murmurs for
all the love and kindness that had
brightened her short married life. No
need to describe the grief that over-
flowed his heart as he told her of how
she had been to him a source of happiness greater than any he could have
given her—deeper and more satisfying
even than his art could breathe into his
soul. A few days, and another gray
stone cross marked in the quiet ceme-
tery the spot where Cicely, after her
short and holy life, slept beside her
father, and another pair of deep blue
eyes gazing into a father's face told

him that Heaven claimed its own, but entrusted to his care another life.

"He named his baby daughter Gretchen; for he could not bear that even his child should bear the name which memory consecrated to his wife.

"As the little Gretchen grew up, her father perceived that her mother's gift of beauty was hers and their united gift of music.

"But here resemblance to either ceased. The touchstone of her nature was ambition. A deep-rooted pride and desire to be foremost in the world's throng, to command homage by her genius—these were her ever-present thoughts; and when cut off from any opening for her cherished plans—for her father refused to allow her at eighteen

years of age to accept the offer of a
director to procure her an engagement
in one of the great capitals of Europe—
she became dissatisfied and discon-
tented with her lot.

"At last, unhappily, her wishes began
to assume reality. As her father waited
for her one evening in the chancel, as
she sang at Vesper service, he observed
a young man, evidently a stranger,
linger after all the worshippers had departed. His air and appearance indi-
cated a high station of life, as well as
they showed his foreign birth. He
looked closely at Gretchen as she
passed, and her father observed that he
followed them home, though at a distance. Thus for many days he watched Gretchen to and from the church,

but always maintaining a most respectful demeanor, until their meeting chanced thus:

"At that time Gretchen was accustomed to go **three** times a week **to the** house of a certain Frau **von** Liessen, **to teach** music **to her three daughters.**

"This lady lived **in a** distant part **of** the city, and Gretchen was accustomed **to** leave her house **whilst it** was still early, and so arrive **at** home before nightfall."

But upon this particular **day** the frau besought her **to** stay, saying that she wished her to sing for **a** number of guests who were even now in the salon. Gretchen at first hesitated, saying that her father would be anxious about her absence, but finally yielded

to the frau's entreaties, as well as to
the promptings of vanity, which whis-
pered that here an opportunity at last
presented itself for winning the laurels
in this aristocratic company which had
already been conferred upon her else-
where.

"Therefore she followed the frau in-
to the large and magnificently-furnish-
ed salon with trembling steps but
proud, triumphant heart. All present
were **touched by her** youthful grace
and beauty, and as she took her place
at the piano a half-audible murmur
of applause broke **the** deep silence.
What nectar so sweet, **what** spur so
effective, as that of applause? Gretchen sang as she had never sung before; higher and more liquid rose the

full notes, until they seemed to rival the harmony of angels.

"Intoxicated with success, and craving the swift, certain applause which she knew would follow each effort, the young girl sang on and never marked the lapse of time, until a servant, entering, lit the numerous waxen tapers which stood in candelabra about the room, and reminded her that it was evening and she was a long distance from home.

"Gretchen had a grateful and affectionate, heart, and, knowing the anxiety which her father would feel at her absence, she reproached herself bitterly for having delayed to such an hour. Hastily approaching an alcove where she saw Frau von Liessen engaged in conversation, she waited impatiently until a suitable opening presented itself, and took leave, saying she must return home at once.

" 'Yes, my dear child,' responded the lady, 'but not alone; it is far too late. My maid Katrina shall accompany you. You can tell her as you pass the housekeeper's room on your way out.'

" Gretchen thanked her and turned to go, when she for the first time saw that a gentleman, the same whom she had so often seen going to and from church, was standing in the alcove watching her.

" Katrina, upon receiving her mistress' message, donned her outdoor garments and led the way into the

street.   An early moon had risen, and
the calm, peaceful light rested upon the
old city, lending it a new and tender
beauty.

"The woman drew her young
charge's arm within hers, and they
hastened along the solitary street.
Suddenly the sound of a quick, firm
footfall came through the stillness,
and in a few moments the same gentleman whom Gretchen had seen in
the alcove a short time before came up
to them, and respectfully uncovering his
head, said gravely: ' Pardon me, fraulein, but it is too late for you to go
through the streets even with this at-
tendant.   I will, with your permission,
attend you home.   Katrina knows me,'
he continued quietly.   ' I am slightly re-

lated to Frau von Liessen, and was her guest at the entertainment this afternoon.'

"Thus reassured, Gretchen walked on between her guardians, and after a little learned to answer in a firm voice the questions which the stranger asked in such deep, quiet tones. Frankly she told him of all her hopes and future plans, of winning by the power of her song the laurel of fame, of her desire to see strange countries and sing to a strange people.

"'Do you think, then, they would welcome you better than the audiences of your own country, fraulein?' he questioned curiously.

"'Yes,' responded the young singer; 'that which we have we never prize so

dearly as when others exult over it.
Those whom we have seen grow up
among us, counted their failures, num-
bered their nearer aimings at success,
do not wring from us that involuntary,
startled admiration that is the tribute to
a new-comer's perfect work. We have
been too near, and watched the painful
ascent, the repeated falls, and treacherous slips, and though we respect the
toiler for his victory, we see no magic
in its execution.'

"'Think you, then,' said the stranger
hastily, ' that the ties of race and blood
and country are so easily broken ? To
me it seems, fraulein, these should but
add another charm to find favor in a
people's heart, and nowhere, in my es-
timation, should a singer's tones rise

grander or with truer ring than in the spot where first was felt the heaven-born power. Home sanctifies all ordinary gifts.'

" 'But the heritage of song is not an ordinary gift, and cannot be judged by the heart's ordinary rules,' said Gretchen hastily. 'See,' she continued, for they stood now upon the low wooden bridge which forded the narrow river—'see! this river, flowing so quietly to the sea, reflects to-night, as it has every starry night since its first flow, Orion's shining belt. Did God to-morrow place it in another hemisphere, it would reflect the Southern Cross as brilliantly within its bosom. Thus is the heart of a singer. The people who welcome and crown her she reflects in her heart's depths.'

"As she stood thus, grasping with one slight hand the wooden rail and pointing with the other outstretched arm to the constellation she had first named, the bell from a neighboring tower tolled the hour of eight. In the momentary stillness that ensued the lapping of the water sounded faint but clear beneath the bridge; then Gretchen, startled, turned, exclaiming: 'Alas! Katrina, I knew not that the time fled so fast. The hour is later by half than I thought, and we must make haste.'

"The remaining distance, however, to Gretchen's home was but short and soon traversed. Her father met them at the door, and after hearing the unex-

pected incidents of the day, thanked
the gentleman for his kindness, assur-
ing him that he had laid him under a
deep obligation.

" ' If you really wish to repay me for
a simple act of duty,' said the stranger
gravely, 'permit me to come here
sometimes and hear your daughter
sing. It is a favor I would value mere
than you imagine.'

" Dreading to appear ungrateful, and
yet with a vague presentiment of trouble, the father gave the requested permission, and the stranger, after a few
more courteous words, departed. The
following evening he returned, and listened with undiminished pleasure to
song after song which Gretchen poured
forth in the still, moonlit room. And

so for many months he came each evening to the old house, and listened as
silently as if he sat indeed at the feet
of music's Muse herself.

"When he first came he had given
his name as Raymond, and told them
that he was an Englishman. Further
than this they enquired not; but, as
they came to know him better, and
time had rendered his presence familiar, the stranger's grave, earnest' manner and noble appearance inspired
deep trust in both.   Gretchen soon
learned to watch for his coming—the
one whose applause was never stinted
and whose criticism never sounded
harsh—and by degrees her father relaxed the vigilance with which at first
he had marked their meeting.

" He often withdrew to the balcony by the open lattice, and there smoked his evening pipe as he listened to Gretchen's songs, recalling days long past when another voice as sweet, if not so grand, awoke his heart to love.

" One still, sultry evening he had retired to the farther end of the balcony from the open window, endeavoring to catch the faint breeze which floated fitfully over the city, and there sat absorbed in deep reverie. In the quiet room Gretchen sat at the piano, her hands idly wandering over the white keys, forming deep, echoing chords at will. Herr Raymond sat near her, but without expressing any wish to hear her sing as usual. A deep preoccupation seemed to engross his mind, and it was a long time before he looked up and said :

" 'Fraulein, you have sung for many nights for me ; have you never had any curiosity to know the name of one to whom you have given so much pleasure ?'

" ' You told my father at first that you were Herr Raymond, and I have always thought since that was your name,' replied the young girl.

" 'No, Gretchen,' he answered, ' my first name is Raymond, but my whole name is Raymond Vane. Now, try to say it as I do.'

" 'Raymond Vane,' repeated the young girl, the unfamiliar sounds falling in broken musical utterances from the smiling mouth.

"'That is right,' he said encouragingly; 'and now, little Gretchen, listen, for I have something very important to ask you.'

"'To ask me, Herr Raymond?' questioned **Gretchen** in a tone of wonder. 'Of what use can I, a poor, obscure girl, be to one so great and rich as you?'

"'**Of** more use than any one in the world, strange **as** you think **it,** little one,' he answered. 'You know, Gretchen, **I am an** Englishman. **My** father and mother are **both** dead, and I was an only child. Far **off, in** one of England's beauty-famed counties, stands my inheritance, **a** grand old manor, shut in on every side by the sweeping glades of an English **park,** and overshadowed by ancient

oaks and spreading elms.   Such is my
home, which has waited. silent and
lonely for my coming for many years.
But I could not bear to return and live
among scenes with the memory of the
dead alone to bear me company.   I
had resolved to. lead the wandering
kind of life which I have pursued since
my mother's death, until one evening,
as I sat in the cathedral near by, I
heard your voice rise in the Vesper
service, sweet and clear.   So remark-
able a voice even in this favored land
attracted me, and soon I grew to love
its possessor for herself.   Gretchen,' he
continued, raising her right hand as it
hung listless by her side, 'do you love
me well enough to leave your fatherland and be my wife ?'

"It was **as** if Gretchen stood in a flood of sunlight stronger than human eyes could bear when those words fell upon her wondering ears. **The** knowledge that she held for the moment the direction of her life in **her** own hands, mingled with the surprise of the offer of marriage from one whom, even in her wildest dreams, she had never invested with such **a wish,** almost stunned her. Raymond Vane, seeing her agitation, **begged** her to speak of it no more that night, and determined **to** address her father next morning.

"What need to prolong the details **of** the stranger's wooing? What entreaties will save the flower from the ruthless hand that is stretched out to rend **it** from the parent stem, or who can convince the flower that in the humble garden of its birth happiness is nearer than in the brilliant places which it is plucked to adorn?

"After a time of tears and regrets checkered by bright anticipations with which hope painted the future, the day came for Gretchen to cut those ties which on this earth were never to be reunited. Before the high altar of the familiar cathedral the simple, humble German girl stood, the bride of the rich and noble Englishman, and that day's twilight, which saw them on the sea embarked for his ancestral home, saw her sorrowing father seated in the old home, where time had shown him so many changes, only to make him again as lonely as upon the day when he had come, friendless and weary, to the city gates.

"The days wore into weeks, the months hastened by, **and** only once brought tidings from his darling—telling much of the place and people, and their ways and customs, but allowing little to be gathered of the happiness of her life. This did not serve to quiet the fears which so unlikely **a** union had raised in his heart. He knew Gretchen had always been of an eager, communicative disposition, quick to relate her happiness to those she loved; and therefore, as the year closed and another went through its course, his fears grew into certainty that the bait which had lured his darling from him had not drawn her into happier places. Each

day he faithfully fulfilled his duties as
capellmeister, but, as he led the choir,
amid the mingling voices hers seemed
to rise, not with the brilliancy which
had distinguished it of old, but with a
murmur of soft entreaty, as if the call
of one in sorrow. Now in the evening
his reveries were of Gretchen ; he
knew the dead was happy, but for the
living he mourned.

"At last, after two years had gone
by, the father sat in his accustomed
place one evening, and turned over
and over in his mind a project which
had seized him with intolerable longing—to go and seek his daughter. If
she should be happy, if her silence
should prove only a natural forgetful-
ness of things below her present sta-

tion, he would retrace his **steps** and trouble her **no** longer ; but if she pined for her old German home, and starved amid a strange people for the **bread of** familiar **voices and** faces, he would bring her back at any cost.

"After **the** night which **saw this** determination recorded **in** the cappel- meister's will, **the dawn** was but break- **ing upon the old** German **city** as he, restless **and unable** to sleep, left his dwelling **to roam** about its familiar streets. But **as** he descended the steps his attention was immediately at- tracted by what seemed a large bundle, **but** upon examination proved to be a **sl**eeping infant. It needed not the paper on its breast to tell him whose it was ; the sleeping features were Gretchen's own. So had she lain in his arms full many times. So did Providence guide her child to that safe resting-place.

"With deep emotion he pressed the child to his heart and carried it into the house; then with eager haste he unfastened the little missive and read the following, blurred with tears:

"'MY FATHER: The daisy is happiest in the field, the violet in the lowly shadow; therefore I confide my Margaret to you. Teach her, as you taught me, how to be contented, and may your counsel prove more successful in her life than it did in mine. Farewell, my loved father! Do not seek me to restore the precious gift. I give it for the best. I have been nearer to you than you imagined, but now am gone for ever.'

"'Your unhappy daughter,

"'GRETCHEN VANE.'

"Such was the only clue which the young mother left to the web of her troubled life. Her father with religious care, took the trust she had given him, and once again began at the beginning of a young life. With the care of a faithful nurse, the little one, too young to know its loss, grew strong and well, and smiled with all its mother's beauty in answer to his caressing words. Only one injunction he disregarded of the message. As soon as the child was old enough to travel he sought its mother in all likely places. But in vain; and at length, when, after leaving the child and nurse in London, he had journeyed to the manor-house only to learn that Raymond Vane and his wife had gone abroad for many years, he became disheartened, and determined to seek in a strange land a home for a time at least. Many reasons aided him in making up his mind to this step. The old German home recalled, with terrible earnestness, the memory of Gretchen; if it was sanctified by the memory of Cicely, it was darkened by Gretchen's unhappiness. Then, again, Margaret was not his; at any day she might be recalled to her father's house, for whatever strange reason she had been given to his care, and he wished that she might not feel the change so keenly as his poor Gretchen. To en-

sure this he took up **his** residence in
a land where the language would be
the same **as** her father's, and **the** customs not so violently opposed. London, or even **the country parts of England**, would have **been better still for**
this preparation, **but the old** man felt
he **could** not bear them. The wild,
majestic beauty **of a** half-settled coun-
try in the **New World better** suited his
artist soul, **and** the change of scene and
active life afforded him less time for
sad reflection. Leaving matters, therefore, **so arranged that his poor** Gret-
chen might, in case **of** need, be able to
communicate with him, he turned his
face towards the new country and soon
found himself settled amid the strange
scenes of the land which he had chosen.

Here seven long years went by without the call from the Old World for
which he patiently waited. 'But at last,
my little Gretchen,' he exclaimed joy-
fully, 'the silence has been broken;
thy mother stretches out her beseeching hands for her father's help. In
this letter, my child,' he continued,
'Gretchen tells me that the tie which
held her to her English home has been
broken, her husband is dead, and she
crosses the ocean to seek me and her
child. By the date she must have
even now arrived; so to-morrow I will
go for my poor child, and in a short
time, my little one, thy mother shall
hold thee in her arms.'"

The amazement, joy, and wonder of
Gretchen may be imagined. To learn

that her mother was living, that she was soon to meet her, were indeed joyful tidings ; but the knowledge of her unhappiness made her grieve in unison with the past.

The next morning broke fair and mild as one of May's fair month of days, and the old man departed on his glad journey, with the earnest prayers and wishes of Gretchen and Frederika for its success.

After the excitement of departure had subsided the long hours of the day grew weary, as time always does to those who sit and wait. To Gretchen it seemed as if noon would never come, and when midday rested upon the still, white-clad land her eager heart sighed for the distant evening.

Thus four days went by, and on the
fifth, which broke in all the wild fury
and pitiless pelting of a winter storm in
that unsheltered region, poor little
Gretchen's resolution to be patient suf-
fered a severe trial.

Seating herself with her work in the
deep window which commanded the
best view of the road from the town,
she spent the early hours of the day,
but without having her watchfulness
rewarded by the sight of a single
passer-by.

At dinner, which she hardly tasted,
Frederika strove to console her by
telling her that it was not yet time;
that perhaps the ship had not arrived;
or, even if her mother had come, a lady
like her could not travel in so great a

storm. These attempts of Frederika Gretchen received thankfully, for the child's natural sweetness of disposition always **led her** to appreciate an offered kindness; but they were **not** effective otherwise. **Dinner** over, she resumed a station by **the** window, and **after** a while sat wholly silent, her hands clasped **in** her lap, fascinated by the scene without, making **to** it **a** pretty contrasting picture in the old window, with her warm crimson dress and curling golden hair.

At last the blue eyes, which turned so steadfastly towards the distant town, were rewarded by the sight of a traveller on horseback. From the first point which afforded a glimpse of him **the** child watched the horse as he picked his steps along the sunken, muddy road, and her astonishment was great at seeing his rider turn him towards their gateway. Summoning Frederika to the window, they both watched him pass through and approach the farm-house. Then, leaping from the saddle, he addressed Frederika, who had by this time opened the door, and stood, regardless of the storm, bareheaded upon the threshold.

Without entering the messenger briefly communicated his news. He had gone into the town in haste for the doctor for his child, who had been suddenly taken ill, but upon arriving at his house learnt that he was absent at the scene of a disaster which had taken place that morning. The stage from

A—— had met with an accident within a mile or **two** of the town, being
upset over a high bank, and most of
the passengers injured, the greater
number but slightly, but **a few** very
seriously. Among these latter was
Jakob Dietz. The deep groan which
Frederika gave from her honest heart
at this awful news was almost lost in
the quick, sharp scream of anguish
which broke from Gretchen, followed
by an agony of childish sobs.

Meanwhile Frederika stood silent
and helpless, uncertain what **to** do or
how to act. The man, who had waited
for some decision or resolve, as we
generally do from those to whom we
communicate tidings that call for im-
mediate action, finally, touched by

the despairing look in her face, said
kindly:

"Perhaps, mistress, you would like
to go to the old man at once.   Now,
I'll tell you what I'll do: I have medicine here for the little fellow, which will
keep him easy until I can go in for the
doctor with another horse and wagon,
for his is broken down.   Now, if you're
ready in an hour, I'll stop for you, and
take you into the town to the house
where he is, and you can stay and
nurse him until he's able to be brought
home."

Frederika thanked him in broken
English, and he, with a hearty "All
right," was turning to go, when Gretchen rushed forward and grasped his
sleeve:

" Tell me," she said passionately "was the one with my grandfather hurt, or is she dead ? Don't be afraid to tell me."

" With your grandfather ?" echoed the man, surprised. "There was no one with him that I heard of."

"A strange lady, she means," explained Frederika, who for the moment had forgotten the old man's expected companion, "whom she expected with her grandfather."

" Well," rejoined the man, " I can't say positively, but all the names I heard of those in the accident belonged to people I know. It seems to me, too," he added, "that I'd have heard is there'd been a strange lady hurt. Anyhow, I wouldn't fret for her," he

continued consolingly, " till I knew
for certain she came and was hurt."

Then, with a last injunction to the
old woman to be ready punctually, he
rode away, and the two entered the
house with their sorrow, and longing
again for the state of feverish impa-
tience and weary waiting of the morning.

For, let argue who will, certainty is
more horrible than the most cruel sus-
pense.   For while the latter lasts im-
agination may as often picture a happy result as paint the most woful end-
ing, with equal probability of being
right.   Events, to be sure, are rarely
so horrible or so perfectly happy as
that powerful magician of our soul
would make them; she often assumes

the appearance of her sister, Reality, but mimics and exaggerates her doings so that when the sober sister shows us the substance it **rarely** affects us as deeply as has the shadow, **but** the difference which gives the pain or joy is that, while we may and must appeal from the decision of the one, we can grasp **the** joy which Reality places in our hands, and must bear the burden of sorrow which she places upon us. And little Gretchen, **bending** beneath its unaccustomed weight, thought happiness was gone for **ever.**

Burying her face in her hands, **she** sat in the window-seat and sobbed on, unheeding Frederika's preparations for departure until, startled by an exclamation from that faithful soul, she raised

her eyes and saw her contemplating
her with an expression of solemn wonder.

"Well, what is it, Frederika?" inter-
rogated the child in a choking voice.
"What is the matter?   Mr. Clark
surely hasn't come back yet?"

"No, but I'm thinking, my little one,"
said the old woman wistfully, "what
is to become of you?"

"Of me!" repeated the child. "Alas!
I never thought of that."   Then, springing up from her recumbent position,
she put her arms round the old woman and continued bravely: "I know,
Frederika, that I cannot go with you;
I would be of no use, and grandfather,
if he knew it, would not want me. But
do not force me to go over to Mr.

Clark's house. I do not like to be
with children when I feel so sad, and
you know I am not used to their ways.
Let me stay here with Fritz; he will
take good care of me, and to-morrow
you will bring grandfather home."

The objections which the old woman
raised to this scheme were overruled.
Fritz, to be sure, was still a most
formidable protector, the house was
well secured in the way of bolts and
bars, and the state of the country was
quiet; and above all she knew that
the child was very shy and was never
happy with those of her own age.

After this understanding the child
repressed her grief somewhat, and assisted her nurse in the preparations for
departure. Mr. Clark soon arrived,

and Gretchen saw her drive away after
loading her with a hundred messages
to her grandfather, and receiving a
solemn assurance from Frederika that
she should be sent for, if nothing else
were possible, in the morning.

With a brave bearing the child wav-
ed her hand for the last time to the
old woman, and then, with a lonely, deserted feeling, closed and barred the
door and seated herself once more in
the window. For a long time she
wept unrestrainedly, until from very
exhaustion she fell asleep. When she
awoke the short afternoon was fast fad-
ing into twilight. The rain had ceased,
but the wind blew with awful violence
and rocked the stout old house to its
foundations. The sun had gone down,

but from west to east there stretched around the earth a belt of lurid light, rendering still more desolate the murky gray of earth and sky. With a start of surprise the child sprang up, and first attended to the fire, which, under such kindly care, soon burnt brightly. Then, opening the window, she, with some difficulty in the face of the furious wind, pulled in the heavy shutters and barred them with a sense of relief at closing out the desolate view and driving wind, which howled as if in pursuit. This accomplished, she drew out the table from the wall into the middle of the room; she lit the lamp, and by its cheerful rays proceeded to set the table for two, for, she argued " Fritz shall share my supper with me to-night, as there are only we two."

As much to divert her mind as from desire for food, she proceeded to prepare it, and the hot, savory odor rising from the fire soon drew Fritz from his corner to the hearth. He seemed to notice the absence of her guardians and to be determined that every attention on his part should be offered to atone for it, licking her hand with fervor at every opportunity and regarding her with an almost human expression in his deep, grave eyes. Supper over, of which he appropriated by far the greater portion, he stretched his huge length before the leaping blaze, and followed Gretchen with his eyes as she washed the dishes and cleared away the remains of the meal. Then, coming **over to the** fire, **she** took her accustomed low seat and drew out her little white rosary. "I will say it as often **as I can** until **I become sleepy,"** she resolved, "and **I** will divide the three parts of each; the 'Joyful' shall be for my mother, that we may meet again; the 'Sorrowful' that God may pity my grandfather's sufferings; and the 'Glorious' that I may be resigned above all things **to his** will." Then, pressing her little crucifix to her lips, she was soon absorbed **in** earnest prayer. The dog watched for **a** time the beads drop **from** her fingers, and then, apparently convinced that she was happy, closed his eyes and slumbered quietly at her feet, with his

head resting upon his outstretched fore-
paws.

It was a charming **picture in the**
long, low-roofed room, swept and gar-
nished into such perfect cleanliness:
the open, generous fire dancing **in**
merry light upon the floor, which ri-
valled unsullied snow in whiteness, now
gleaming on the polished tins and shin-
ing delf upon the walls, then resting on
the fair, sweet face of Gretchen, framed
in flowing, golden hair, tinting **her** dress
with deeper crimson, and beaming upon
the great animal at her feet until his
eyes sparkled like gems in black setting.

The ticking **of** the great Dutch
clock, which loudly marked Time's flight
in the deep **silence,** had finally tolled

the hour of ten. Gretchen looked at its broad, **familiar face,** in amazement at the lateness of the hour, and rose **immediately** to retire, when a quick motion from the hound **at** her feet made her pause. Thus they remained for the moment—the child, with blanched face, turned towards the door, and the dog with his massive head thrown back and his eyes angrily watching in an attitude of the most profound attention. In another like brief space Gretchen fancied that in spite of the wind, which had somewhat lulled, she heard a footstep, and this idea was confirmed by the loud and furious baying of the hound, who sprang up and flew to the door, snarling and showing his teeth savagely.

Gretchen, terrified, fell on her knees speechless at the horror of her situation, but in her heart vehemently entreating God's protection.

Suddenly there came from without a cry for help as of nature's last despairing effort, piercing the air with awful sharpness. At that sound Gretchen sprang with a bound from her knees to the door and pulled back its heavy bolts, the dog close to her side. At last the door swung open, and Gretchen saw crouched against the door-step the form of a woman which an instinct, almost an inspiration, told her was her mother.

"O my mother!" she cried in her joy, "have you come at last?" And stooping, she lifted the wanderer in her young, strong arms.

Thus assisted, **her** mother entered the house which had so long awaited her, and, with the weariness of death upon her limbs, sank into the great arm-chair which Gretchen pulled **be-fore** the fire.

The faintness which had seized **her was** partially dispelled by the drops of brandy which Gretchen hastened to administer, and the mother was enabled to contemplate the face of her child, and found her to be what her imaginings had pictured **her—a** repetition **of** her own grace and beauty, but with a heart untouched by ambition or yearnings for else beside the gifts that God had given.

" Tell me, my Gretchen," she said in **the old,** familiar tongue of Fatherland, "what hast thou thought of thy mother's absence from her child—that she was cold and ungrateful for so great a blessing ? "

" No, never that, mother," replied the child. " I only knew I had a mother when grandfather told me you were coming; and he said that you would tell me why you stayed so long away."

"And so I will, my little one," replied the mother, " that it may prove to thee that God knows best, and places us in this life, not where we love most, but where we best may serve him.   I forgot this, my child, and reaped the bitter harvest of sorrow and of sin which my own hand had sowed.   I left my humble station and my kind father to fulfil the brilliant future which my dreams had pictured me. But, ah! my God," she exclaimed, shaken with remorse, "I purchased earthly happiness at a fearful price. **Thy** father, my child," she continued, **"was not** of my faith and violently opposed to it. **He had** married me, fondly hoping that my youth and timidity would quickly yield to his love and influence. The horror with which I recoiled from the first shock against my religion made him pause, but not relent. **He tried** in vain to shake my faith by irony and ridicule, but the supernatural gift was beyond his human power; he, therefore, appealed to my will by every means at his command, and after many struggles **I** finally yielded and consented to deny my God.

"But, like all sinners, from that hour
remorse poisoned every drop of happiness.   Sleeping or waking, I seemed to
hear a voice within my heart reproach-
ing me as one who, like Judas, had betrayed my Lord for a miserable pit-
tance.   At last, my Gretchen, when
thou wast laid within my arms, I resolved that my sin should not rob thee
of thy best inheritance.   Therefore I
had thee secretly baptized, and as soon
as an opportunity offered left thee to
my father's care.   I could not meet him
and tell him the awful truth ; I rather
left him in ignorance of the strange
cause which placed thee in his protect-
ing arms.   During the search which
ensued, the many strange surmises, as
to thy disappearance never came near

the truth, and we returned to England only to leave it again after a dissatisfied residence of a few months. Three more years passed, and then in sunny Naples an infant son **was** given to us. My husband, proud and **joyful**, returned to England, and, as the baby grew into a boy, devoted himself to his education. And truly, Gretchen, thy brother was indeed almost peerless in his bright, boyish beauty and grace of bearing. Even **I** forgot for a while my sin, and at times fancied myself happy. But this state, a hundred-fold worse than the first, was destined to be shattered by one of those awful blows with which God tears asunder the veil which our guilty hands have woven to conceal him from us.

"One clear, bright autumn day I stood upon the terrace of my husband's mansion and watched him and our boy go towards the lake for a sail—an amusement of which little Raymond was particularly fond. Two hours later their bodies, locked in the cold embrace of death, were taken from its treacherous depths. A sudden squall, preceding a violent shower of rain, had overtaken the little boat when crowded with sail at some distance from the shore, and before assistance could reach them both had perished.

"O God! my child, may you never know the anguish of an hour when, crushed with awful woe, you are afraid to call on God to lighten it or give you strength to bear it. Prostrate I lay,

unable to roll away the stone my im-
pious hands had placed at the door of
my heart, and afraid to look upon the
face of the angel Sorrow, whom he had
sent in mercy.

"Such was the agony to which I
awoke from a deep swoon upon hearing the awful tidings, which I endured
until all funeral rites were paid, and
the dead slept in the family vault their
long, still sleep; then, like a guilty
thing, I fled in the night from the para-
dise my act had poisoned. Without
purpose or direction, I wandered until
I came to London, and there, exhaust-
ed in body and mind, fell sick of a fe-
ver. The woman in whose lodgings I
was taken ill proved in truth a good
Samaritan, and when, after long deli-

rium, I woke, a priest was by my bed-side, and my confession brought relief to my tortured soul.   As soon as I was able I resolved to come to my poor father and you, my child, and according-ly embarked on my long voyage. Weary with travel, I arrived in the town to-night and enquired the direction, but could find no conveyance to bring me to my destination.

"The longing which filled my heart to see you, my child, grew maddening, when, conscious that only a few miles separated us, I set out to walk, but on the way encountered a teamster, who offered me a seat in his wagon, which I gladly accepted, for I felt that I had begun a hopeless undertaking.

"When we reached a turn in the

road just below, the man pointed out the light to me, apologizing for being unable to bring me any further, as the roads were very heavy and up-hill. I thanked him, and, giving him some money, alighted and commenced my painful walk. At last I reached the threshold, but there sank half-fainting on the door-step. After a while I roused myself to give a cry for help. You heard and came."

Gretchen then explained to her mother why her grandfather and nurse were absent, but added she was sure they would return on the morrow. With deep interest her mother enquired about the accident, but the child could give her only the meagre intelligence which Mr. Clark had brought.

As Gretchen sat at her mother's feet, gazing upon the wan, worn beauty of that sad face, she observed that the excitement of their meeting had subsided and left her still weaker than before. Her face, even to her lips, was deathly white, and she pressed at intervals her hand upon her side, as if in pain.

Finally, yielding to the child's entreaties, her mother determined to retire, and Gretchen showed her to her room and assisted her in preparations for the night, for her weakness was gradually growing worse.

Then, extinguishing the light, she lay down beside her. For a long time she kept awake, listening to the faint, irregular breathing of her mother; but at last, tired and worn out by the exciting events of the day, she fell asleep.

She was roused towards morning by a feeble groan, and, springing from bed, rushed to her mother's side, and screamed in terror as she saw her face changed and distorted by a violent spasm.

" Mother! O mother! what shall I do?" she cried. "Are you dying? Oh! speak to me. Tell me what I can do for you."

In a few moments the features relaxed and the spasms subsided. Her mother asked for a small bottle which she would find in the pocket of her dress, and upon the administration of a few drops seemed much relieved. She was enabled to speak,

and held the child by the hand as
she cried:

"Gretchen, I am dying; I feel it and
know it by this awful pain here," press·
ing her heart. "I knew it must end
my life soon, but this journey has
hastened it. Only one thing troubles
me: I must die without the sacraments.
Therefore I would like you to read the
prayers for the dying in case I am unable to speak to you when the last hour
comes. Will you, my child, control
your grief and do this?"

As her mother uttered this request
in broken, gasping sentences, Gretchen
had sobbed bitterly, but now she raised
her head and said bravely:

"Surely, mother, God will not take
you from me so soon. I will pray to

him and he will make you strong
again. But, however," she continued,
as her mother shook her head feebly,
"you can see a priest easily. He does
not live far, and I can go for him and
bring him back."

The expression of joy which came
over her mother's face told Gretchen
how much her promise had relieved
her. She therefore determined to go
immediately. Kneeling down, she fer-
vently begged God to grant her
mother's wish, and, if it were his will
that she must die, not to summon her
unstrengthened by his holy aids. Then,
arranging the medicine within easy
reach of the sufferer, she arrayed herself in warm outdoor garments and
softly drew the heavy bolts.

Summoning Fritz to follow her, she
threw it open and stepped out into the
cold, gray morning.

The priest's house lay close to the
church, which was a couple of miles
distant by the road, but within a few
moments' access if one crossed the
brook. Gretchen, therefore, determined upon taking this course, and a few
moments' brisk walking brought her to
its banks ; but she shrank terrified at
its awful aspect.   Wide and deep, it
swept with an angry rushing against
the banks it had caressed in summer.
The faces of the six large stones used
to ford it were just visible where their
dark, wet surface rose at intervals from
its raging bosom, and the child saw
that to cross it would be a hazardous un-

dertaking. Still, she was not deterred.
Remembering her important errand, she
murmured **a devout** ejaculation **to** that
Mother for whom, through **all** the years
of her child-life, she had cherished a
great and peculiar love ; **then,** placing
one foot upon the nearest stone, she
cautiously endeavored to reach **the**
next **at a** comparatively still moment,
and in this way succeeded, in spite of **a**
few slips, in reaching the other shore with
no worse mishap than a pair of wet feet.
Looking back, she saw that Fritz **had**
been unable **to** emulate her courage,
and stood wistfully regarding her from
the opposite bank, but **afraid to risk his**
aged limbs in the swift current. Knowing that it was useless to coax him to
try what his affection could not

prompt him to undertake, she hastened
on her way and soon arrived at the
priest's house.

The housekeeper informed her that
he had only just returned from a very
distant sick-call, and was resting, but
took her message, and returned with
the answer that he would come immediately.

Refusing the housekeeper's invita-
tion to take a cup of coffee which she
was preparing, Gretchen hastened on
her way home, and soon arrived at the
perilous crossing.　Fritz, from his station on the opposite side, wagged his
tail and testified great joy at seeing
her return.

The child placed her foot upon the
stone, but found this crossing much

more difficult. A strong wind blew in
her face, and she was cold and numb
with fatigue **and** hunger. She was
seized with an awful dizziness, and terrified with the thunderous rushing
which resounded **in her** ears. She
made a spring, but missed, and in **one**
instant **was** at the mercy of the cruel
waters.

Her piercing shriek was echoed **by**
a frantic howl from Fritz, who sprang
to the rescue of his beloved little mistress, but in vain. **H**is strength was
unequal to his noble intention, **and in**
that cold, gray **dawn**, which heralded
to the earth another day, the angry,
foaming waves closed upon the child
and her intended preserver.

·   ·   ·   ·   ·

There remains **but** little to be told.
The **priest soon** arrived at the farm-
house, and, finding **that the** child
had not returned, suspected **the fatal**
truth.　Summoning assistance to the
dying woman's bedside, **he departed**
for the town, there meeting Frederika
and **the** old man just setting out for
the farm-house.　Jakob Dietz's injuries
were not as serious as had been at first
supposed.　At first he listened to the
tidings of the priest in silence, and
bowed his white head in submission to
the divine decree which only permitted
the loved wanderer **to** return to die
within his arms ; but when he went on
to speak of the fate which he feared .
had overtaken his grandchild, his human love rose rampant against the

hand which had **cut so** dear a tie from his solitary, lonely life.

The priest, **a** man singularly gifted with penetration, wisely forbore to even lightly touch **so raw a** wound; therefore, only cautioning Frederika **to** be cautious in telling the awful news to the mother, he departed, and the two so stricken in years and sorrow set out for their desolate home.

The gorgeous sunset **of** the cold winter's day had turned all the small diamond-paned windows of the old house to deepest crimson color, when the priest slowly drove up to the door.

Entering, he noticed an unusual hush and reverence among many people moving about, and, advancing into the large household room, he saw upon a bier, in all the cold marble perfection of that mysterious Sculptor's works, the body of little Gretchen, with a sweet, calm expression upon the childish face, as of one who had gladly thrown off old garments to draw round her the priceless robe of immortality.

Near her bier sat the old man, regarding with a passionate expression of grief the image of his darling. The priest drew near and questioned him about the mother, but received only the shortest possible replies. Every faculty seemed numbed with woe, and the priest could see that his heart was far from being resigned to the will of God.

"Jakob Dietz," he said solemnly,

" will you, then, after following Jesus so
patiently through all his suffering way,
refuse to take the last step? Will you,
like a few unhappy ones among the
martyrs, refuse to suffer the last pang,
and so lose the merit of all that
had gone before? Happiness is often a weight which chains us here;
sorrow and suffering the wings by
which we rise to the crown which
God sets in the heavens. Will you not
be generous and give when God holds
out his hands?"

The old man, startled by this sudden exposition of his secret thoughts,
was recalled from his wandering to
that narrow path of self-sacrifice in
which, from early youth, his feet had
trodden. Without a word he rose,

pressed his lips to the forehead of the beautiful corpse, and led **the** way to the bedside of the mother. She rested quietly and calmly, worn out by violent spasms, and waiting calmly for the end, which came even **as the priest** stood by her bedside, and, like the **clear sunset of a gray** and troubled day, foretold a happy morrow.

. **In the still,** quiet graveyard on the hillside **the** long, green summer grass **waves** against the white **cross which** marks the spot **where** Gretchen **and** her mother rest, almost within sound of **the** brook which the child had so loved **in life, and** which brought **her** so cruel **a death.** The old **man and** Frederika still dwell within **the old** house, now sanctified **to** them **by** the memory of the beloved dead, and not far from the house Fritz lies buried, where a rude shield rising from the ground bears the record of his noble act, thus honoring a dog of whom it might be truly said "that he possessed beauty without vanity, strength without insolence, and courage without ferocity."

THE END.

www.ingramcontent.com/pod-product-compliance
Lightning Source LLC
Chambersburg PA
CBHW032202010726
47493CB00008BA/2793